FAYE AND SPOT

T.S. Cherry

Faye And Spot

Every child learns to read music and books in different ways and at his or her own speed. You can help your young musician improve and become more confident by encouraging his or her own interest and ability . From the books your child reads with you to the first books he or she reads alone, there are Read and Play books for every stage of reading:

Ideal for Sharing with Emergent Readers
Basic language, Poems, Rhymes, word repetition, and whimsical character illustrations, ideal for sharing with your emergent reader

Reading with help
Short sentences, familiar words, and simple concepts for children eager to read on their own.

Reading with little help
Engaging stories, longer sentences, and language play for developing readers.

Reading alone
Complex plots, challenging vocabulary, and high-interest topics for the independent reader

Advanced reading
Short paragraphs, chapters, and exciting themes for the perfect bridge to chapter books.

Visit popacademyofmusic.com for more information

Copyright © 2013 T.S. Cherry
Editor: Brenda Walker
All rights reserved.
ISBN/SKU:9780996163149
ISBN Complete:9780996163149
Imprint Name: Pop Academy of Music

The Lines of the Bass Clef

 Fifth Line

 Fourth Line

 Third Line

 Second Line

 First Line

 First Line below the staff

3

5

7

2

4

6

Locate the **Lines** piano key.

Read and Play!

SPOT

2

Faye has a dog
That can fit in her hand
He's yellow with spots
And he's become her best friend

He came from a flower
As the story is told

He was touched by an Angel
Saved by Faye Row

He came from up high
And that's all that we know

He just fell from the sky
And into the snow

Onto a patch of flowers
Barely visible she saw his nose

It's a miracle she said
It's a dog, and he glows

Faye found him in the forest
Buried beneath the snow

Alight all around him
As tiny as a bow

So she brought him home
And gave him a bath

In a bowl made for soup
It was all that she had

She made him a collar
From a bracelet she found
No one was using it
It was just lying around

She wrapped him in a washcloth
And handled him with care

As she decided what to name him
And brushed his short hair

Faye knew, yes she knew
Just what she must do
She held him close and said
I'll take care of you
Doggy
Treats!!!

She called him Spot!
He could fit in her hand
He found a new home
With Faye his new friend

www.ingramcontent.com/pod-product-compliance
Lightning Source LLC
Chambersburg PA
CBHW071015120726
47910CB00004B/1527